Lizzie McGuire

Broken Hearts

Adapted by Kiki Thorpe
Based on the series created by Terri Minsky
Part One is based on a teleplay written
by Melissa Gould.
Part Two is based on a teleplay written
by Terri Minsky.

EGMONT

First published in the USA 2003 by Disney Press
Published in Great Britain 2004
by Egmont Books Limited
239 Kensington High Street, London W8 6SA

Published by arrangement with Disney Press,
114 Fifth Avenue, New York, New York 10011-5690

ISBN 1 4052 0514 8

5 7 9 10 8 6 4

A CIP catalogue record for this title is available
from the British Library

Printed and bound in the UK

PART ONE

CHAPTER ONE

It was Saturday night, and the Digital Bean café was hopping. Lizzie and Miranda leaned on the counter, watching the crowd and waiting for their fruit smoothies. Lizzie had ordered a *grande*-size Strawberry-Banana Mania, and Miranda was getting a Pineapple Parfait. In just a few hours, the scary movie marathon would be on TV, and Lizzie and Miranda could hardly wait.

"I hope they show the one where the

zombies wake up, take over the radio station, and play bad disco music," Lizzie said excitedly. Talk about spooky! After watching that movie, Lizzie hadn't been able to look at her parents' record collection for weeks.

"Or the one where those newlyweds realize that their honeymoon is actually a *horror-moon*," Miranda added.

"The scary movie marathon rocks," Lizzie said. "Gordo doesn't know what he's missing."

"Yeah," Miranda agreed. "He must like his dad a lot, because he didn't seem too bummed to have to spend time 'bonding' with him."

Lizzie rolled her eyes and groaned. "Bonding" was one of those weird things parents came up with to torture their kids. For one afternoon, your dad stopped being your dad and tried to act like your best friend instead. It was supposed to make you feel closer, but to Lizzie it was just further evidence that men are from Mars, women are from Venus, and parents are from *Pluto*.

"The last time me and my Dad 'bonded,' I got stung by a bee," Lizzie said. They'd been on a picnic when a bee dive-bombed Lizzie's nose like there was a bull's-eye painted on the end of it. It had taken two days for the swelling to go down. It was like her own personal scary movie marathon, Lizzie thought: *Attack of the Killer Bees* followed by *Lizzie the Red-Nosed Teenager*.

"Oh, yeah?" Miranda said. "Well, the last time my dad and I bonded, I almost broke my toe!"

Lizzie shuddered, remembering. Miranda had to spend an entire afternoon with her foot propped up on pillows after her dad Rollerbladed over her toes. The only thing she bonded with that day was an ice pack.

Ding! The service bell rang. The girl behind

the counter pushed two tall takeout cups toward them.

"Yup," Miranda said as they picked up their order. "I think it's much safer staying at home and getting scared out of our brains."

Sipping their drinks, Lizzie and Miranda turned to leave. Then, suddenly, Miranda grabbed Lizzie's sleeve and tugged her back.

"Uh, correct me if I'm wrong," Miranda whispered. "But are Gordo's dad and Brooke Baker the same person?"

"Huh?" Lizzie asked.

Miranda pointed to the other side of the café, where Gordo was sitting at a little table. In the seat next to him, wearing a purple sweater and a big smile, was Brooke Baker, a girl from their science class.

Lizzie blinked. She'd never seen Gordo sitting so close to any girl but herself or Miranda. It was weird, she thought, seeing him so chummy with Brooke. She felt like she was looking at one of those silly, mixed-up drawings where people's clothes are on backward or the sun is shining at night, and you have to figure out *what's wrong with this picture?*

"He and his dad must've rescheduled," Lizzie told Miranda. "He obviously came here looking for us."

Miranda looked skeptically at Gordo and Brooke. "He doesn't *look* like he's looking for us," she replied. "He looks like he's on a . . ." She wrinkled her nose. "I can't even say it."

"Say what?" asked Lizzie.

"*Look* at them," Miranda said. "Private table. Away from the crowd. Sitting close." She narrowed her gaze. "Gordo even looks like he brushed his hair!"

"So?" asked Lizzie.

"*So?*" Miranda raised her eyebrows meaningfully.

"Oh, please," Lizzie scoffed. "You don't think they're on a *date*, do you?"

Miranda pursed her lips as if that was exactly what she thought.

"No way," Lizzie said. "It's Gordo, remember? We're his best friends. He would have mentioned it."

They watched as Brooke tipped back her head and laughed at something Gordo was saying. He *would* have mentioned something as important as a date, Lizzie told herself. Wouldn't he?

"Come on," she said. "Let's go get him."

Sipping her Pineapple Parfait smoothie, Miranda reluctantly followed Lizzie through the crowded café. But they had taken only a few steps when Gordo suddenly set down his cup, leaned forward, and—

Lizzie stopped dead in her tracks. Miranda spit out a mouthful of smoothie.

Gordo and Brooke were kissing.

"Or maybe we should go," Lizzie said. It was like watching a car wreck, Lizzie thought as Gordo pressed his lips against Brooke's again. She knew she shouldn't look, but she couldn't tear her eyes away.

Miranda's eyes were practically bugging out of her head. "Gordo just kissed someone," she gasped. She looked down at the half-empty drink in her hand. "I'm not sure, but I think I just lost my appetite."

Miranda grabbed Lizzie's arm, and they ran for the door. But as they left, Lizzie glanced back over her shoulder, sneaking one last look at Gordo and Brooke.

"Gordo's got a girlfriend! And i thought the movie marathon was going to be scary."

* * *

Early Monday morning, Lizzie and her brother Matt sat side by side at the kitchen table, silently spooning cereal into their mouths. Now and then, Matt nibbled at his toast, or Lizzie took a sip of orange juice. It seemed like a peaceful morning in a perfectly normal household.

Which was why Mr. and Mrs. McGuire were worried. They stood together at the kitchen counter, studying their children.

"It's awfully quiet," Mr. McGuire whispered to his wife.

"I know," she whispered back. "One of them must have done something."

"I'll take Matt. Lizzie's yours," Mr. McGuire suggested.

"Deal," said Mrs. McGuire. Picking up the sack lunch she'd just made, she walked over to her daughter.

"Here's your lunch, sweetie," Mrs. McGuire declared cheerfully. She handed the bag to Lizzie.

Lizzie glanced at the bag. "Thanks, Mom," she said quietly.

"I cut off the crusts like you like," Mrs. McGuire added with an encouraging smile.

"Great," Lizzie said.

"And I put an extra snack in there, too."

"Great," Lizzie said again.

Mrs. McGuire didn't move. She hovered next to Lizzie, staring her down like a lion waiting to pounce on a mouse. Lizzie glanced sideways at her, and calmly took another sip of orange juice. She was used to her mother's interrogation tactics.

At last Mrs. McGuire couldn't stand it anymore. "Okay," she said, "what happened?"

Lizzie turned and looked at her mother. *What happened?*

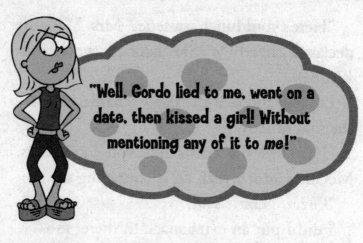

"Well, Gordo lied to me, went on a date, then kissed a girl! Without mentioning any of it to *me*!"

"Nothing," Lizzie told her mother. "Really." Somehow discussing Gordo's lip-lock over a bowl of oatmeal didn't seem like the key to a well-balanced, nutritious breakfast.

"Nothing?" Mrs. McGuire said. "Everything's okay at school? With your friends?"

"Yeah," Lizzie said. "Fine." Pushing her chair back from the table, she smiled at her mother, picked up her lunch, and left the room.

"Hmm," Mrs. McGuire said to Lizzie's

retreating back. Defeated, she walked back to the counter where Mr. McGuire was calmly sipping a cup of coffee. He smirked.

"Watch the pro," he whispered to Mrs. McGuire. He walked over to the table, and sat down in Lizzie's empty chair.

"Hiya, Matt," he said casually.

"Hiya, Dad," Matt replied, without looking up from his cereal.

Mr. McGuire nodded and sipped his coffee. For a long moment, they sat together in silence.

At last Matt turned and looked curiously at his father. "What's going on?" he asked.

Mr. McGuire shrugged. "Nothing. How 'bout with you?"

Matt sighed. "Well," he said, "I think I have a science test, but I'm not entirely sure. I kicked our social studies globe last week by accident, and now I have to work in the cafeteria to help pay for a new one. And I totally don't know what's going on in math."

Mr. McGuire nodded again. "You got a lot on your plate, son," he said.

"Yup," said Matt.

"How 'bout I help you with your homework after school?" asked Mr. McGuire.

"Cool," said Matt.

"Cool." Mr. McGuire slid his chair away from the table and walked back to his wife, triumphant.

Mrs. McGuire folded her arms and pursed her lips. "Hmph," she said.

CHAPTER TWO

Dressed in safety goggles and rubber gloves, Lizzie and Gordo peered down at the spongy, gray blob in the tray in front of them. As Lizzie watched, Gordo carefully lifted a corner and began to slice. Their science class was doing a unit on sea life, and today they were dissecting a squid. That is, *Gordo* was dissecting a squid. Lizzie was trying hard not to be sick.

"So how was the scary movie marathon?" Gordo asked as he sawed at a tentacle.

"Scary," Lizzie said, vowing never to eat calamari again.

"My dad and I got home too late to watch it," Gordo told her.

"Really?" Lizzie tried to sound surprised. "What did you end up doing instead?"

"We went to a book signing," Gordo replied, without missing a beat. "The guy who wrote it spent six months walking across the Himalayas. He started out with nothing but a pair of shoes and a candy bar."

Lizzie gritted her teeth. Not only was Gordo telling her a big, fat lie, he had the nerve to make it sound like the truth!

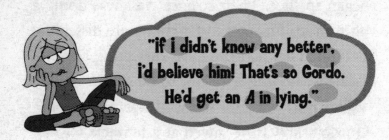

"Sounds interesting," she said carefully, wondering just how far Gordo would take his lie. But before she could ask more about his evening with his "dad," the girl at the next lab table suddenly slipped a note into Gordo's hand.

Wiping his hands on his lab coat, Gordo turned his back to Lizzie and unfolded it. As his eyes skimmed the page, two pink spots appeared on his cheeks. He turned and looked toward the back of the classroom.

"Who's it from?" Lizzie asked, trying to peer over Gordo's shoulder. But she already knew. She followed Gordo's gaze to the back table where Brooke was sitting with Claire, one of the snottiest cheerleaders in the eighth grade. Brooke giggled and waved at Gordo.

"Um, Lizzie, you seem to have everything under control," Gordo said suddenly, holding the squid out to her. "Uh, I'll be right back."

"Gordo, you cannot just leave me with this dead octopus!" Lizzie cried. But Gordo was already dumping the slimy thing into her hands.

"Look," he said, handing her the scalpel. "All you have to do is keep slicing. Don't worry if you make a mistake. There are seven more legs."

"Gordo, you're my lab partner!" Lizzie snapped. "You cannot just leave me!"

But apparently he could. Lizzie watched, steaming with anger, as Gordo walked over to Brooke's table. She could almost feel the smoke pouring out of her ears.

"Hello! Hi, there! Hey, i'm your best friend, remember? Over here!"

But it was useless. Lizzie could have been juggling chain saws and wearing a kazoo-playing orangutan on her head, and Gordo still wouldn't have noticed.

"Ooh!" Lizzie clenched her fist angrily. *Squish.* Suddenly, Lizzie realized that she was still holding the squid. *Yuck!* Quickly she dropped the squid back into the pan.

Great, Lizzie thought, casting a final, furious glance in Gordo's direction. Now she'd lost her best friend *and* her science partner.

"Gordo walked away from a *science* project?" Miranda asked in amazement. It was lunchtime, and Lizzie and Miranda were sitting at their usual table, waiting for Gordo. Lizzie glanced quickly around the quad to see if he'd arrived yet. She wanted to fill Miranda in on the entire squid incident before he showed up.

"After he got a note," Lizzie informed Miranda.

"Gordo got a *note*!" Miranda looked like she might choke on her Jell-O.

Lizzie nodded. "And he still hasn't mentioned his date the other night," she added.

"Gordo had a *date*?" Miranda shrieked.

Lizzie put her hand on Miranda's shoulder. "Calm down, Miranda. You were there."

Miranda shook her head. "Sorry," she said. "This whole thing is rocking my world. I mean, Gordo and Brooke are definitely an item. People are *talking*."

"About *Gordo*?" Now it was Lizzie's turn to freak. Since when did anybody ever talk about Gordo?

"i feel like i'm in a dream where everyone wants to kiss my frog!"

"See, here's the part that gets me all Confucius," she told Miranda. "Not that Gordo has a girlfriend . . . but that Gordo is somebody's *boyfriend*."

Miranda wrinkled her nose. "Eww!"

"I know!" Lizzie exclaimed. "Very hard to imagine." She tried to picture Gordo picking Brooke up for a date, Gordo bringing Brooke flowers, Gordo serenading Brooke with a guitar. Nope, Gordo was just *not* boyfriend material.

"I guess if you live long enough, anything can happen," Miranda said, shaking her head.

Just then, Gordo walked up to their table. "Hi, guys," he said. "I just wanted to tell you that I'm not going to be eating lunch with you today."

Lizzie nodded thoughtfully. "Hmm. Interesting," she said.

"Yeah," Gordo went on. "It's just that I

promised a friend that I'd help out with some homework."

"A friend, huh?" Miranda said. Lizzie and Miranda glanced at each other. Since when did Gordo have any other friends?

"Yeah, so"—Gordo scuffed his sneaker against the ground—"I'll see you guys later."

Lifting a hand, he turned and walked away. Lizzie and Miranda watched as he made his way to another table and sat down next to Brooke. She smiled and scooted closer to him.

Miranda narrowed her eyes. "Does he honestly think we don't know?" she exclaimed. "We saw them *kissing*!"

"Maybe they were just talking really close," Lizzie said.

"That wasn't talking," Miranda said.

"Maybe she had a smudge on her mouth or something," Lizzie suggested.

Miranda looked at her in disbelief. "That he was trying to get off with his *lips*?"

"Listen, Miranda, I'm just looking out for him, okay?" Lizzie said. "Gordo is H and H with Brooke. If there's any possibility that Gordo's going to get hurt, we've got to stop it."

The two girls turned and looked back at Gordo. He was hot and heavy with Brooke, all right. And they had to do something. Starting today.

CHAPTER THREE

After school that day, Matt and Mr. McGuire sat at the kitchen table, working on Matt's homework. A gleaming collection of red, white, and blue gum balls sat on the table next to them.

"Okay, Matt," Mr. McGuire said, pointing to a neat row of gum balls. "Each row's got ten gum balls in it. That represents a hundred percent. Now, if we take away the four white ones . . ." Mr. McGuire scooped four of the gum balls into his hand. "What percentage of the gum balls are missing from the row?"

Matt chewed his eraser thoughtfully. "Forty, right?" he said at last.

"Right. Good job. I knew that using gum balls as a visual aid would help." Mr. McGuire patted Matt's shoulder and stood up from the table. "Don't eat your homework," he instructed. "And help me take out the trash."

Matt looked at his father thoughtfully. "Uh, I don't think so," he said.

Mr. McGuire raised his eyebrows. "Excuse me?"

"Dad, I bet there's a one hundred percent chance that you're going to ask me to take out the garbage again," Matt said.

"So?"

"So, if I'm right, I'm not doing it. If I'm wrong, I will," Matt said slyly.

Mr. McGuire frowned, confused. "Matt," he said in a warning tone. "I'm going to ask you one more time. Help me take out the garbage."

"Man, this percentage stuff is easy," Matt said. He popped a gum ball in his mouth and stood up from the table. "I'll be in my room. Thanks again, Dad."

Mr. McGuire watched him leave, scratching his head. He had no clue what had just happened.

Meanwhile, over at the Digital Bean, Lizzie and Miranda were snacking on cupcakes and sipping *grande*-size fruit smoothies, waiting for Gordo to arrive. They'd agreed that it was time to confront him about his secret life as Brooke's boyfriend.

"Next *you'll* be meeting somebody behind my back," Lizzie said to Miranda. "I won't even know until I see you with him. Kissing. And soon you'll be ditching me for him at every single turn. I'll be alone." Lizzie put her hand dramatically to her forehead. "All alone."

Miranda smiled. "Not going to happen."

"It might," Lizzie pointed out. "One day."

"Are you kidding?" Miranda asked. "You'll know all the D."

Lizzie sighed and poked at her cake. Maybe knowing all the dirt on Miranda was possible. Obviously, she'd been clueless with Gordo. "I guess it's too late to have this conversation with Gordo," she said. "Now he's with someone who's completely wrong for him."

Miranda shrugged. "Maybe Brooke really likes Gordo," she said. "I mean, sure, he's a little different. But that's why *I* like him."

Lizzie's eyes opened wide. "*You* like Gordo?" she said with a gasp.

"No!" Miranda said quickly. "I don't *like* him like him. You know what I mean." Suddenly, she turned and stared at Lizzie. "Wait, do *you* like Gordo?"

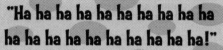

"Ha ha ha ha ha ha ha ha ha ha
ha ha ha ha ha ha ha ha ha ha!"

"No!" Lizzie exclaimed. She definitely did
not like Gordo . . . did she? "At least, I don't
think so," she added. After all, Gordo was the
smartest guy she knew. And they always had
fun together. And he was kind of cute, in his
own way. . . .

Lizzie felt a moment of panic. What if she
really *did* like Gordo? Would she tell him?
Would they go out . . . on a *date*? She tried to
imagine Gordo standing on her doorstep,
holding a bouquet of roses.

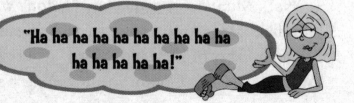
"Ha ha ha ha ha ha ha ha ha ha
ha ha ha ha ha!"

Nope. Lizzie breathed a sigh of relief. Gordo was definitely not boyfriend material.

"Of course I don't like Gordo," she said loudly. "Gross!"

"Just asking," Miranda said, right as Gordo walked up to them. Miranda pinched Lizzie, and the two girls grinned at him. *Nope, we weren't talking about you. Not us. Uh-uh.*

"Hey," Gordo said. "I'm glad you guys are here. I wanted to tell you something—"

"Well, we wanted to tell you something, too," Lizzie interrupted. "And there's no easy way to say this, but, uh, we know about you and Brooke."

"Oh." Gordo looked surprised. "That's exactly what I wanted to tell you guys about."

But before he could say more, Lizzie cut him off again. "We kind of saw you two together, and don't take this the wrong way, but . . ." She paused and looked Gordo in the eye. "Have you ever thought that maybe she's using you?"

Gordo's face drew back as if he'd been slapped. "Is there a right way to take that?" he asked.

"You bailed on me in science," Lizzie said, suddenly feeling angry. "Then at lunch, to help her with her homework. And I know I saw you two kissing–"

Miranda held up her hand, cutting Lizzie off. "I'm still trying to cleanse the memory," she said.

Gordo looked back and forth between them. "You saw us here the other night?" he asked.

"We're best friends," Lizzie said. "I can't believe you haven't mentioned her. Not once."

"Well, I'm sorry if I wanted to keep

something in my life private," Gordo said.

"We're just trying to help you, Gordo," Lizzie said. "We're protecting you. We don't want you to get hurt."

"By telling me she's using me? Why? Because a girl like Brooke could never like a guy like me?" Gordo's green eyes darkened with anger. "Well, guess what? She does."

"It's just that it's *Brooke Baker*," Miranda blurted out. "I mean, she's friends with Claire—that's all we're saying. . . ."

"She's also friends with me," Gordo snapped. "In fact, we're more than friends. . . ." He stopped and shook his head. "Funny, I came here to tell you guys how happy I am, thinking you'd be glad for me. I guess that's just too much to expect from my best friends. See you around." Turning on his heel, Gordo stormed out the door.

"Gordo, wait," Lizzie said. But he was already

gone. With a jingle of the bell, the door swung shut behind him.

Miranda and Lizzie looked guiltily at each other. They had the sinking suspicion they'd just made a *grande*-size mistake.

"Why do I have the feeling that Gordo just broke up with us?" Miranda asked.

Lizzie sighed and looked at the door. "'Cause he did," she answered.

CHAPTER FOUR

By Tuesday afternoon, Matt had gone from math flunky to math junkie. After school, he sat in the kitchen, discussing his newest hobby with his friend Lanny. A heaping mound of lollipops, jawbreakers, sour taffy, fruit chews, and mini chocolate bars sat on the table between them.

"Okay, Lanny," Matt said. "This is how it's going to work. Every time *I* guess right, I'll take one percent of all the candy here. Every time I guess wrong, *I'll* take one percent of all the candy here."

Lanny rolled his eyes.

How could he have ever thought math was hard? Matt wondered. It was a piece of cake. Or make that, a piece of candy.

Just then, Lizzie walked into the kitchen. Without looking at Matt or Lanny, she opened the refrigerator and took out a pitcher of orange juice.

"Here she comes," Matt whispered to Lanny. "Okay, I'll bet you all the candy here that Lizzie starts yelling at me."

Lanny nodded.

As Lizzie began to pour a glass of juice, Matt picked up a jawbreaker and hurled it at her. It bounced off her shoulder.

"Ow!" Lizzie hollered. She spun around and glared at Matt. "I thought I told you that between the hours of twelve noon and twelve noon, you're supposed to ignore me!" she yelled.

Matt blinked innocently. "But you never said I couldn't throw things at you," he pointed out.

"Aaaargh!" Lizzie groaned in frustration. Grabbing her glass of juice, she stomped out of the room. Matt wrapped his arms around the pile of candy and pulled it toward him.

Suddenly, Lanny grinned and waved his arms. Matt's eyes lit up. Lanny didn't talk much, but somehow Matt always knew exactly what he was saying.

"That's a great idea, Lanny!" he cried. "We'll play Odds and Percentages at school, but with other people's candy. Sweet!"

Matt's mind began to churn. If he played his cards right, he could triple his investment, he thought. Or quadruple it. Or whatever came after quadruple. He'd be king! Matt imagined himself standing atop a mountain of gummi bears, bubble gum, and chocolate bars. He chuckled and rubbed his hands together greedily.

On Friday, Gordo still wasn't speaking to Lizzie and Miranda. All that week, Lizzie had gone out of her way to pass by his locker, but he never seemed to be there. And when she saw him in class, he acted like she was invisible. Even in science, where Gordo and Lizzie were supposedly partners, Lizzie couldn't make eye contact with him. If Gordo wasn't standing at Brooke's lab table, he was staring at her like she was some kind of fascinating petri-dish experiment.

"This is the longest I've gone without talking to Gordo since he deliberately smushed my brownie in the third grade," Lizzie said miserably, as she and Miranda walked out of math class.

"How long did your fight last then?" Miranda asked.

"Till the bus ride home," Lizzie replied.

Miranda sighed. "Well, maybe this is what happens when your best friend is a boy," she said. "Things get complicated."

"I guess," Lizzie agreed sadly. "I just miss him."

"You can try talking to him," Miranda suggested. "I hear he waits for Brooke at her locker between classes."

Lizzie stared at Miranda. "Gordo waits at her locker?"

"He's in a relationship now," Miranda pointed out. "It's sort of required."

Lizzie was about to say something more, when a loud voice drowned out her thought. She looked up and saw Claire walking down the hallway with a group of cheer-leaders.

"Tomorrow night?" Claire was saying. "Coolie. But first I've got to help Brooke get ready for her hot date. It's at the Holy Rigatoni. Isn't that romantic?"

Lizzie turned to Miranda. "*Hot date?*" she repeated.

"Gordo's her boyfriend," Miranda replied. "Wrap your mind around it."

Lizzie shook her head. "Hot date and Gordo are never used in the same sentence! Especially by Claire," she said. "Brooke's date is obviously with someone else." If Gordo didn't know anything about this hot date, Lizzie thought, then that was proof that Brooke was totally two-timing him. And there was only one way to find out for sure.

As soon as their next class was over, Lizzie and Miranda hurried over to Brooke's locker.

Sure enough, Gordo was standing there, holding Brooke's books. Lizzie pulled him aside.

"So, Gordo, I'm really sorry about what I said," she said. "And I've decided to be totally supportive of you and Brooke." Lizzie smiled convincingly. She wasn't quite sure how to bring up Brooke's "hot date," but that sounded like a good start.

"You have?" Gordo said.

"Yes," Lizzie went on. "Because it seems like you really like each other. And I'm sure when you two are together, it's . . . very cool."

"Only, not cool," Miranda jumped in. "More on the . . . *warmish* side?"

"Even warmer than warm?" Lizzie added. She and Miranda looked at Gordo expectantly.

Gordo's brow wrinkled in confusion. "What's warmer than warm? What are you guys talking about?" he asked.

"David!" Brooke suddenly called from down the hall. She waved impatiently at Gordo. "Hurry, we're gonna be late for science!"

Lizzie and Miranda looked at each other and raised their eyebrows. *David?* Nobody called Gordo by his first name—except maybe his grandmother.

Gordo turned to Lizzie and Miranda. "I gotta go," he said. Lizzie and Miranda watched as Brooke and "David" walked off to science class, arm in arm.

"There," Miranda said to Lizzie. "You happy now?"

"No, Miranda, I'm not," Lizzie replied. "Gordo had no clue about this 'hot date.'"

Miranda snorted. "Well, I wouldn't either with the way that conversation was going."

But Lizzie didn't seem to hear her. "I was right," she said. "Brooke is two-timing Gordo. She's gonna totally destroy him."

"Lizzie," Miranda said calmly, "unless you actually *go* to the Holy Rigatoni, *spy* on Brooke, and get *pictures* of her date, then you have nothing."

Lizzie's face brightened. "That's it!" she cried. "We'll spy. We'll do it for Gordo. Brilliant idea, Miranda."

"That's not what I meant!" Miranda cried. "And we are *not* spying."

Lizzie looked her friend in the eye. "Yes," she said firmly, "we *are*."

CHAPTER FIVE

By Saturday evening, the McGuires' phone was ringing off the hook. Odds and Percentages was a raging success at school, and Matt was the chief bookie. He strode around the living room, taking calls on the cordless, while Lanny scribbled notes in a pocket-sized notebook.

"What I'm saying is there's a one out of five chance Mr. Broadwell's going to be wearing his Beers of the World tie on Monday," Matt explained to his thirtieth caller that evening. "You're either in on the action or you're not. . . ."

"I'm in, I'm in!" cried the kid on the other end of the line. Quickly he placed his bet.

Matt listened, nodding, then cupped his hand over the receiver. "Put Joel down for two pudding packs on Broadwell," he told Lanny. Suddenly, he heard the click of Call Waiting. Matt's face lit up. "Ooh, another call," he purred. "Hello?"

"What time tomorrow?" the caller asked. Matt recognized the voice of a fifth grader named Josh Bynder.

"The dodge ball game's tomorrow at two," Matt told him. "Odds are two to one that blue's gonna crush yellow."

Josh told Matt he would wager his skateboard helmet on yellow.

"Throw your kneepads in with the helmet, and you got yourself a deal," Matt told him.

"Bet my helmet on yellow," Josh said again, before hanging up.

"Put Bynder on yellow," Matt shouted to Lanny. The phone clicked again. "Ooh, another call," said Matt. He glanced over Lanny's shoulder. "How we doin'?"

Lanny held up the notebook. Page after page was filled with the names of Matt's classmates and the items they had bet: yo-yos, sodas, Frisbees, pudding packs, sunglasses, CDs, bubble gum, baseball cards . . . the list went on and on. Matt smiled.

"Other people's candy," he murmured happily as he clicked over to the other line. "Yo!" he shouted into the phone. "Talk to me."

Lizzie stood in the entrance of the Holy Rigatoni, anxiously looking around. The lights in the restaurant were dim, and candles in little glass jars flickered on the tables.

Delicious smells wafted through the air, but Lizzie couldn't even think about eating. She was so nervous, she almost felt like she was on a *real* date.

She turned to ask Miranda if she could see Brooke. But Miranda wasn't there.

"Come on, Miranda!" Lizzie groaned. She yanked open the door and dragged Miranda inside by the elbow.

Miranda looked sullenly at Lizzie. She was wearing a blue button-down shirt, a yellow tie, and an old corduroy blazer that they'd found at the back of Mr. McGuire's closet. Her long brown hair was tucked up inside a tweed cap.

"Why am I the one dressed like a boy?" she complained.

"Because your voice is deeper," Lizzie told her. "Besides, you know this was your idea."

"No, it wasn't," Miranda shot back. "And I'm having a big problem, Lizzie. I have to go to the bathroom."

"So, go."

Miranda pointed to the doors labeled LADIES and GENTS. "Which one?" she snapped.

"Oh," Lizzie said. "I see your problem."

Suddenly, Miranda gasped. "There's Brooke! There's Brooke!" she cried. She grabbed Lizzie and ducked for cover behind a large potted plant.

Lizzie peeped though the leaves. She could see Brooke talking to someone, but the plant was blocking his face.

"I can't tell who she's with," Lizzie said. "Wait, he's getting up!"

"Who?" asked Miranda.

"Her date!" Lizzie cried. She watched the boy's legs as he walked toward the rest room.

"He's going to the men's room," she reported to Miranda. "Go, follow him!"

Miranda looked at the door marked GENTS. "In there?" she asked in horror.

"You said you had to go," Lizzie said. "So go!"

Miranda shook her head. "I can't go in there," she said. "They have those weird fountain thingies on the walls!"

"Go!" Lizzie said. She gave Miranda a little push. Miranda shot Lizzie a "you owe me one" look over her shoulder. Then, pinching her nose, she pushed open the GENTS door.

Lizzie crouched lower behind the plant, trying to imagine who Brooke's date could be. Maybe it was Tony, the red-haired soccer player who had a different girlfriend every week. Or maybe it was that tall guy, Jason, whose locker was across the hall from Brooke's. I bet it's someone that Claire set her up with, Lizzie thought. That would be just like Claire—

Lizzie's thoughts were suddenly interrupted as Miranda came flying out of the men's room. "We've got to get out of here!" she yelped. She grabbed Lizzie's arm and began pulling her toward the door.

"Why?" Lizzie asked, shaking Miranda's hand off. What was the rush, when they were about to find out that Brooke's date was . . .

Gordo! Lizzie whimpered as the door to the men's room swung open and Gordo walked out. So Gordo was Brooke's hot date, after all! And if he saw Lizzie and Miranda here, he would be more than hot—he'd be steaming mad!

"Come on, go!" Miranda cried, shoving Lizzie toward the door. The girls turned to flee.

But just as they reached the door, the restaurant host stepped in front of them.

"Hey, thanks for waiting," he said cheerfully. "Your table's ready."

Miranda's eyes widened with alarm. She looked at Lizzie and shook her head. "Oh, we're not staying," Lizzie told the host quickly. "Thank you."

But the host blocked their path. "Sure you are," he replied. "First dates make me nervous, too." He looked at Miranda and added, "Cute couple."

"What do we do?" Miranda whispered into Lizzie's ear.

Thinking fast, Lizzie grabbed two menus away from a couple at a nearby table and passed one to Miranda. They held the menus up in front of their faces as the host led them past Brooke's table.

"Right this way," the host said. To Lizzie's

and Miranda's horror, he sat them in a booth right next to Gordo and Brooke. Quickly, the girls slid into their seats and slouched low.

"While you wait for your server, may I suggest an appetizer?" the host asked. "I'd recommend our Ooey-Gooey Extra-Chewy Mozzarella Marinara Madness. Or our Large-and-In-Charge Artichoke Barge with Perfect Parmesan Puffs."

"Uh, yes," Lizzie said, only half listening.

"Fine," Miranda said. She glanced over just in time to see Gordo return to his table.

As the host walked away, Lizzie glared at Miranda. "We could've made a run for it!" she hissed.

"No, we couldn't!" Miranda hissed back. "Gordo is right there. He would've seen us!" She looked around desperately. "What are we going to do?"

"What are we doing to do? We're gonna sit

here and wait for the food that we ordered! We do have to pay for it, you know," Lizzie snapped.

Meanwhile, at the next table over, Gordo had a dilemma of his own. Brooke had a string of pizza cheese stuck to her lip—and he didn't know how to tell her.

"I really like this restaurant," Brooke said. She took another bite of pizza and chewed happily.

"Yeah. Me, too," Gordo said. He pointed at the corner of her mouth. "Um, you have a little—"

"I also really like being here with you," Brooke said, oblivious to Gordo's gestures. "I wish we'd spend more time together."

"We're together now," Gordo pointed out. He touched the corner of his own mouth, hoping Brooke would catch on. "There's a—"

"But more time together would be

awesome," Brooke said. She smiled at Gordo. The string of cheese quivered on her lip like a small antenna.

"Cheese," Gordo finished helplessly. It was useless. Brooke wasn't paying any attention. Gordo sighed. "Well, I mean, we're together in between classes," he said. "We're together during classes. We're generally together after school. Unless I transferred into *all* of your classes—"

"Could you?" Brooke said quickly. "I mean, it's not too late in the semester?"

She smiled hopefully at Gordo. Gordo looked into her lovely brown eyes. Suddenly, he knew what he had to do.

From the next table over, Lizzie watched Gordo and Brooke gaze into each other's eyes.

"Fine, I was wrong," she told Miranda. "Gordo *is* her hot date."

"*Thank you*," Miranda said. She breathed a sigh of relief. "*Now* can we go?"

Lizzie pulled out her wallet and placed some money on the table. "This should cover the food. Come on." She glanced over at Gordo. "They're talking now. They won't see us leave."

"Wait!" Miranda said as Lizzie stood up. "Whose idea was it to come here *really*?"

"Fine, mine. Whatever." Lizzie rolled her eyes. "Come on!"

Lizzie and Miranda slipped out of their booth and sprinted toward the door. But they didn't see the waiter coming toward them, carrying a tray piled high with food.

Crash! Lizzie and Miranda slammed into the waiter, knocking the tray from his hands. Tossed salad and spaghetti and meatballs flew through the air, and the girls tumbled backward onto the floor. A second later, Lizzie and

Miranda were lying on their backs, covered head to toe in spaghetti and tomato sauce. The entire restaurant turned to stare at them.

"Oh, sorry," Lizzie said weakly.

"Hey, isn't that Lizzie?" she suddenly heard Brooke say. "Her date looks a lot like Miranda."

"That's because it *is* Miranda," Gordo replied angrily. Miranda's cheeks turned the color of marinara sauce. She looked mortified.

Suddenly, the host was looming over them. From the look on his face, Lizzie could tell he didn't think they were such a "cute couple" anymore.

"Oh, we're really sorry," Lizzie said. "Um, my friend's not feeling very well, and I've got this thing I've got to go do. . . ." Her mouth felt like it was running on autopilot, and it was coming in for a crash landing!

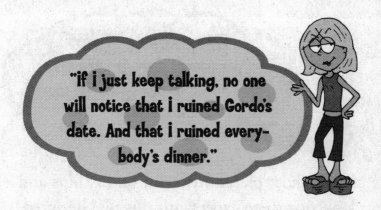

"if i just keep talking, no one will notice that i ruined Gordo's date. And that i ruined everybody's dinner."

"Boy, this place is crowded," Lizzie babbled on. "You guys sell a lot of those Artichoke Barges here, huh?"

"Are you done yet?" the host snapped.

But before Lizzie could answer, Gordo was suddenly standing next to the host. He gazed at Lizzie and Miranda with a look of disgust.

"No, they can't be done," he said angrily. "They have the rest of my life to destroy. This is just one night of it. Come on, Brooke." He took Brooke's hand, and the two left the restaurant.

"Gordo's right. I've done permanent damage here. As permanent as this spaghetti stuck in my hair."

The host placed his hand on his hips and looked at them expectantly. "Well?" he asked.

Lizzie's mouth opened and closed soundlessly. Miranda ran a finger across the sauce on her face and licked it. "Oh, way too much garlic," she said in a low, boylike voice.

Everyone turned to stare at her. Miranda chuckled nervously.

"Guess we'll take this stuff to go," she added.

CHAPTER SIX

Sunday afternoon, Mrs. McGuire stood in the living room, sorting the week's laundry into piles of Dirty, Really Dirty, and Biohazard. You learned a lot of things about your family doing the laundry, Mrs. McGuire thought. She picked up one of Lizzie's shirts with the tips of her fingers. The shirt was splattered top to bottom with what looked like spaghetti sauce. Mrs. McGuire shook her head, and dropped it into the Biohazard pile. She didn't even want to know.

As Mrs. McGuire picked up a pair of Matt's jeans, a small black notebook fell from the pocket. She picked it up curiously, and flipped open to a random page.

"'Four point spread on second period soccer game . . .'" she read. Mrs. McGuire turned another page and read, "'Kids who owe me stuff: Scotty—pack of gum. Kim—clean my scooter.'"

At that moment, Matt and Lanny walked in the back door, carrying backpacks stuffed with toys, candy, and sports equipment. Matt jumped when he saw his mother. A guilty smile spread across his face.

"Oh. Hiya, Mom," he said brightly.

"Hiya, Matt," said Mrs. McGuire. She held up the notebook. "I found your book."

"So I *did* leave that at home!" Matt blurted. "I mean," he added quickly, "that's not mine."

Mrs. McGurie folded her arms. "Care to explain this to me?"

Matt glanced at Lanny. "Uh, not really," he said.

"Have you boys been gambling?" Mrs. McGuire asked.

Suddenly, Lanny set down his backpack and ran out the back door like his heels were on fire. Matt smiled nervously at his mother.

"I love you, Mommy," he said sweetly.

"Matt? *Matt?*" Mrs. McGuire's voice rose several decibels. "Talk to me. I'm waiting."

Matt sighed. He might as well tell the truth, he thought. Or at least one version of it. "See, it all started with this percentage stuff we were learning at school," he explained. "I wasn't really getting it, so Dad explained it in a way that—"

"Matt! Don't blame this on your father," Mrs. McGuire broke in. "I mean, I know he can be a little . . ." She shook off the thought and fixed Matt with a steely look. "No. Never mind. Go on, go on."

"So, then I helped explain it to everyone else," Matt said. "And the next thing you know, people were so . . ." Matt paused, searching for the right words. A bead of sweat trickled down his brow. "*Thankful* for my help," he continued. "They started giving me all this stuff." He set the loaded backpack down on the table. A black-and-white puppy crawled out. It stared up at Mrs. McGuire, panting happily.

Mrs. McGuire scooped up the puppy and scratched it behind the ears. "That's a very nice story, honey," she said to Matt. "But I'm not buying it."

"But, Mom, I'm providing a service to the people!" Matt exclaimed.

"A service?" Mrs. McGuire's eyebrows

looked like they might shoot off the top of her head. "Honey, you were lying, cheating, and gambling."

Matt gave her a hurt look. "Okay, so maybe I did lie," he admitted. "And, sure, you can throw in gambling. But I, Matt McGuire, am not a cheater." Matt placed his hands over his heart and looked innocently at his mother.

"Well, good," Mrs. McGuire said, unmoved by his performance. "Then you'll be very fair when you return all these 'gifts' everybody gave you."

"If you say so," he said reluctantly.

"Oh, I say so," Mrs. McGuire replied. "See, this is a zero-spread situation, and you are one hundred percent busted. I think you understand me." She leaned forward and dumped the puppy into Matt's arms. "Return the puppy."

The puppy whimpered. Matt pressed it to

his cheek and gave Mrs. McGuire his best pleading, puppy-dog look.

"Sorry." Mrs. McGuire shook her head. "Don't go there."

Out in the McGuires' backyard, Lizzie and Miranda sat on the deck, glumly crumbling a plate of chocolate-chip cookies into little pieces. Somehow knowing that Gordo was mad at them made their favorite snack taste like sawdust. They hadn't heard a word from him all day, and they'd been too afraid to call him.

"If I never see another meatball again, I'll be happy," Miranda remarked. "Do you know how long it took me to wash the smell of garlic off my hair?"

"I guess it's just the two of us now," Lizzie said. "No more Gordo."

"No more Gordo," Miranda murmured.

"No more long lectures about how we care

too much about what other people think about us," Lizzie said.

"No more useless information about stuff we never even cared about in the first place," Miranda added.

Lizzie smiled sadly. "No more packs of cupcakes to share," she said.

"No more cupcakes—wait, why not?" Miranda asked.

"'Cause they come in packs of threes," Lizzie explained. "There's only two of us now. I guess we could split the third one. . . ." She thought for a moment, then shook her head. "No, it still wouldn't be the same."

Suddenly, they heard a voice say, "Hey."

Lizzie and Miranda looked up in surprise as Gordo walked into Lizzie's backyard.

"Hi," said Lizzie. She didn't know whether or not to smile. She didn't want to seem unfriendly, but she didn't want Gordo to think she thought any of this was funny, either. She settled on a sort of half-smile. Gordo didn't smile back.

"What are you doing here?" Miranda asked him.

"Not that we don't want you here," Lizzie added quickly.

"I guess that I just didn't say everything to you that I wanted to last night," Gordo said.

"Oh," Lizzie and Miranda said at once. Lizzie took a deep breath, bracing herself for the worst.

"Honestly," Gordo exclaimed. "I can't believe you guys would go so far as to spy on me and Brooke. That's just really, really low. Especially for you."

"It was Miranda's idea," Lizzie blurted out.

"Lizzie!" Miranda punched her in the arm.

"And I also can't believe that you guys spied on me," Gordo went on.

"You just said that, Gordo," Lizzie said.

"I know," he said. He looked at them for a moment. "On the one hand, I'm really insulted. But on the other, I realize that you guys did it because you care a lot about me."

Lizzie breathed a sigh of relief. Miranda smiled. "Yeah, that's the one," she said.

"Well, for your information, Brooke and I broke up," Gordo said.

"What?" Lizzie yelped. "Is it because of what we did last night? Gordo, I'm really sorry. You've got to get her back. If she won't listen to you, I'll try talking to her—"

"Wait, wait." Gordo held up his hands. "I broke up with her," he told them. "In a lot of ways, Brooke's really great."

"Told you," Miranda muttered to Lizzie.

"She's smart. She smells good. She's easy to be around. . . ."

"So, what's the problem?" Lizzie asked.

Gordo frowned. "It's kind of conceptual," he explained, "but I guess I just like the *idea* of having a girlfriend a lot better than actually *having* one."

Miranda and Lizzie glanced at each other. "Yep, he's back," Miranda declared. No doubt about it, this was one hundred percent Gordo speaking.

"Look," Gordo said. "The kissing was cool, and getting notes was kind of fun. I'm just not ready for that kind of commitment. I had to wait for her by her locker; I had to pay for her lunches. . . ." Gordo shrugged. "I had no time for myself anymore."

"Bummer," said Lizzie. This time, a real smile tugged at the corners of her mouth.

"I also had no time for you guys," Gordo added. "I really missed that part."

"So did we," Lizzie said, letting a full grin spread across her face.

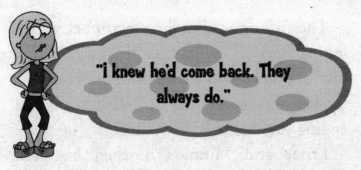

"i knew he'd come back. They always do."

Finally Gordo smiled, too. "So," he said, "interesting wardrobe choice last night, Miranda. Oh, I'm sorry, I should say, *Mirando*."

Miranda groaned and gave Lizzie another punch. "I said it once, and I'll say it again— it wasn't my idea!" she exclaimed.

"So, Gordo, one thing you haven't told us," Lizzie said casually.

"What?" Gordo asked.

Lizzie smiled. "How was the lip-lock?" she asked.

"Sorry, I don't kiss and tell," he said, shaking his head.

The girls jumped to their feet. They weren't letting him off so easy on this one. "Come on," Miranda said. "Spill."

"I'm not gonna do it," Gordo replied, edging toward the gate.

Lizzie and Miranda blocked his path. "Dish, dude," Lizzie said.

She put one arm around Gordo's shoulders, and Miranda put her arm around the other side. Together they made kissing noises in his ears, while Gordo ducked and tried to squirm free. Laughing, Lizzie, Miranda, and Gordo headed off together. Maybe they'd even stop off for a pack of cupcakes.

Lizzie McGUiRE

PART
TWO

CHAPTER ONE

The thing about middle school, Lizzie often thought, was that you only *thought* you were there to learn history and algebra. What you were really being tested on was your ability to survive under harsh social conditions.

"School is actually a reality game show. People get voted out, and just when you think you have the rules figured out, they change."

It began like this: Lizzie was walking to class with Miranda and Gordo. She was listening to Gordo rant on about the grade he'd received on his science project, when she noticed a boy and girl walking with their arms around each other's waists. A second later, Lizzie saw another couple walk by, holding hands.

"A hundred and eighty pounds is good," Gordo complained. "Don't you think if a bridge made out of toothpicks can hold a hundred and eighty pounds, I should get an A? But no. Since Mike Barto's father is an engineer, he brings in a bridge that can support a circus elephant. And I'm left holding a B-plus."

But Lizzie wasn't listening anymore. Near a row of lockers, a boy and girl were talking quietly, their fingers intertwined. Over in the stairwell, a girl was laughing as a boy whispered in her ear. As Lizzie stared at them, another couple walked by with their hands in each other's back pockets.

"Is it just my imagination," Lizzie asked, "or—?"

"No," Miranda said as she looked around in alarm. "When did this happen?"

"I don't know," Lizzie replied. "You know, maybe there was some memo that we didn't get?"

"That's all right," Gordo said loudly. "I wasn't talking."

Lizzie rolled her eyes. Gordo could build an exact model of the Brooklyn Bridge out of toothpicks, but he wouldn't notice the social bandwagon if it rolled over his toe. "Look around, Gordo," she said. "Do you notice anything unusual?"

Even Gordo couldn't help noticing the couples. "Everyone's paired off," he said.

"It's like Noah's ark with fluorescent lighting."

Lizzie and her friends watched as more and more lovebirds filled the hallway. The cuddle craze seemed to be spreading quicker than last winter's flu.

Great, Lizzie thought. Just my luck.

"It's out of nowhere—a school-wide epidemic. The love bug. And everybody's been bitten but Miranda, Gordo, and me."

That afternoon, Matt sat at the McGuires' kitchen table, frantically opening packs of baseball cards. One by one, he ripped off the cellophane, rifled through the contents, and finally tossed the cards into a growing pile.

Matt growled with frustration. He'd spent almost six weeks of allowance on baseball cards, and he still hadn't found the one he wanted.

Finally, he was down to the last pack. Matt clasped it to his chest. Turning his eyes toward the heavens, he pleaded, "Paul O'Neill, Paul O'Neill, please let there be a Paul O'Neill."

Taking a deep breath, Matt tore open the pack and quickly shuffled through the cards.

No Paul O'Neill. With a sigh of disgust, Matt tossed the cards onto the pile of rejects and turned to his parents, who were unloading the dishwasher.

"Dad, I'm going to need an advance on my allowance," Matt said.

"Absolutely not," his mother exclaimed. "He's already well into next year." She frowned at Matt. "Don't think I'm not keeping track, buddy."

"Jo, he's making an investment," Mr. McGuire said, handing her a stack of plates. "You know, my own baseball card collection is worth a small fortune."

"'Small' being the operative word here," Mrs. McGuire replied.

"But Mo-om!" Matt whined. "I only need one more Yankee player and I've got the whole team!"

"That's what they do," Mr. McGuire told him. "They make less of one so you'll buy more cards to try and get it. They're vultures, son, they want to get you by the throat and squeeze you for every penny you're worth."

He glanced over at Mrs. McGuire. As soon as her back was turned, he pulled a five-dollar bill from his pocket and slipped it into Matt's hand. "Don't give up," he whispered.

Just then, Lizzie wandered into the kitchen, talking to Miranda on the cordless phone.

That day at school, Lizzie had counted twenty-two brand-new couples. She needed to compare notes.

"And did you hear about Greg Cable and Stella Vance?" Lizzie asked Miranda.

"No way!" Miranda exclaimed on the other end of the line. "She's like a foot taller than him."

"I know," Lizzie said. "But I saw her in Bio, and she was writing all these notes and dotting her i's with little hearts."

"You know what I think?" Miranda said. "It's a full moon. My mom says weird things always happen when there's a full moon."

That couldn't be it, thought Lizzie. At least she hoped not. She couldn't handle this kind of weirdness twelve times a year. "Or maybe it's because Valentine's Day is next week," she suggested.

Miranda made a sound of disgust. "Who celebrates Valentine's Day?" she asked. "It's, like, the doofiest holiday ever."

"I don't know. Maybe we're supposed to," Lizzie said.

Dingdong. The McGuires' doorbell rang. "Only maybe no one wants to celebrate with us," Lizzie added as she walked over to answer it.

"That's horrible," Miranda said.

"Yep, I bet that's it," Lizzie said. Cradling the phone between her ear and her shoulder, she opened the door.

Ronny Jacobs, the paperboy, was standing on the doorstep. He was a little bit taller than Lizzie, with spiky blond hair and sleepy-looking green eyes. He smiled at Lizzie and held up a piece of paper.

"Collecting," he said.

Lizzie took the phone from her ear. "Moooooom!" she shouted toward the kitchen.

"It's the paperboy." Turning her back to Ronny, she shifted the phone to her other ear. "Face the facts," she told Miranda. "I mean, even Joyce Lutz has a boyfriend. I have to wonder, is there something wrong with me?"

"No!" Miranda told her. "Is there something wrong with me?"

Suddenly, Lizzie felt Ronny's eyes on her back. She turned and saw him looking at her—just a little too closely. Lizzie felt her cheeks grow hot. Had he heard what she had said to Miranda?

"Hold on, okay?" she said into the phone.

"Lizzie, was that a no? Did you say no?" Miranda asked urgently.

Lizzie cupped her hand over the receiver. "Are you *listening* to me?" she asked Ronny.

He gave her a funny look. "Oh, I'm sorry. I forgot to turn my ears off," he said.

Just then, Mr. McGuire hurried into the

front hallway, fumbling with his wallet. He pulled out a few dollars and handed them to Ronny.

"Hey, Ronny. Sorry to keep you waiting," he said.

"No problem," Ronny said, handing him the receipt. "See you next week." He turned to leave. Mr. McGuire was about to close the door behind him, when Lizzie yanked it out of his hand. She had a few things to settle with this nosy paperboy. Passing the phone to her father, she dashed down the steps.

Mr. McGuire held the phone up to his ear. "Lizzie? Was that a no?" he heard Miranda squawk again on the other end of the line.

Lizzie chased Ronny across the front lawn. "Wait a second!" she hollered.

Ronny stopped and turned to look at her. "I have to finish my route," he said. But he didn't move.

"You know, I think it's really rude, eavesdropping like that," Lizzie said when she caught up to him.

"Well, I think it's really rude, ignoring someone in your doorway," Ronny replied.

"Well, it's not like you came to see me," said Lizzie.

"How do you know?"

"What?" Lizzie stared at him.

"How do you know I wasn't here to see you?" Ronny asked.

"Did you come to see me?" Lizzie asked in surprise.

Ronny shook his head and smiled. "No, I was just doing my job," he said. He started to walk down the sidewalk.

Frustrated, Lizzie followed him. "See, now you're giving me a hard time, for absolutely no reason," she said.

"No, there's a reason," Ronny told her.

"Okay, well, what is it?" she asked.

Ronny stopped walking. Lizzie stopped, too. They were standing in front of her neighbor's house. "If you want to find out, you'll have to wait. This is one of my stops," Ronny said, nodding toward the house.

Lizzie folded her arms across her chest. "Fine, then I'll wait," she said.

"You will?" Ronny looked surprised.

Lizzie shrugged. This guy was annoying, but he was also kind of cute, and she was curious about what he was going to say. He'd better have a good reason for giving her this much trouble, Lizzie thought.

"I'll be right back then. Don't move," Ronny said, flustered. "Well, if a car comes, you can move," he added. Ronny started to walk toward the house. Suddenly, he stopped and turned back to Lizzie.

"But to answer your first question," he said,

"there's definitely nothing wrong with you."

Lizzie blinked. For a moment, they stared at each other. Then Ronny turned and sprinted up to the house. Lizzie smiled and gave herself a little squeeze. Maybe this guy wasn't so bad, after all.

CHAPTER TWO

"**O**kay, so what happened to you last night?" Miranda asked Lizzie the next morning as they walked through the quad before school. "You hung up on me, you never called me back—" She stopped when she noticed the weird, dreamy smile on Lizzie's face.

"Okay," Lizzie said. She pulled Miranda over to an empty table and lowered her voice. "I'll only tell you if you agree to *the cone of silence.*"

Miranda traced a cone in the air with her fingers. "We're in *the cone of silence*," she told Lizzie. "Go."

"Okay," Lizzie said breathlessly. "I think . . . maybe . . . I think I like someone."

Miranda rolled her eyes. "Lizzie, everyone knows about your crush on Ethan Craft. Except, maybe, Ethan Craft."

"It's not a crush," Lizzie told her. "And it's not Ethan."

Miranda gasped. "It's not Ethan?"

"No," said Lizzie. "His name is Ronny Jacobs, and he goes to Jefferson. He's cute and funny and he plays the guitar—"

"Wait, wait, wait," Miranda interrupted, holding up her hands. "How do you know someone I don't know?"

"Well, he's our paperboy," Lizzie explained. "But he said he's always wanted to talk to me. And last night he finally did." Lizzie could feel a goofy grin spreading across her face, but she didn't try to stop it. She loved to think that Ronny had noticed her, but he'd been too shy to say anything—it was just so totally romantic.

Just then, Gordo plopped down at the table. "What's going on?" he asked.

"Lizzie's in love with her paperboy," Miranda replied casually.

"Oh," said Gordo.

Lizzie glared at Miranda.

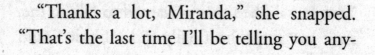

"Cone of silence! Cone of silence! I believe the words are self-explanatory!"

"Thanks a lot, Miranda," she snapped. "That's the last time I'll be telling you anything." Scooping up her books, Lizzie stomped off to class.

That afternoon, Matt lay on the grass in the local park, thumbing through the binder that contained his baseball card collection. Every time he came to the empty spot where Paul O'Neill's card should have been, he felt a pain in his heart. Without O'Neill, his entire collection was worthless.

Oscar and Reggie, two boys from his class, lay on the grass next to him. They both had their own binders of baseball cards open in front of them. Oscar and Reggie were two of the best collectors in the fifth grade, and this afternoon Matt was hoping to do some serious trading.

"Anybody got Paul O'Neill?" Matt asked hopefully. "I'm ready to give away the store."

"I got Jeter," said Oscar.

"I got Clemens," Reggie said.

Matt groaned. He was starting to think the Paul O'Neill card was just a myth someone made up to torture ten-year-old boys, when suddenly he heard a voice overhead say, "I've got O'Neill."

Matt looked up. Standing above him was a small, blond girl from their class named Melina. She held open a purple three-ring binder of baseball cards. In the center of the page, the Paul O'Neill gleamed like an exotic jewel.

Matt stared, dazzled by its brilliance. "It exists," he said worshipfully. He reached out to touch it.

Snap! Melina shut the binder on Matt's hand. "Ouch," she said coolly as Matt yanked his finger free. She tucked the binder under her arm and turned to walk away.

"Fifty cards!" Matt cried. "I'll give you fifty cards for Paul O'Neill."

Oscar and Reggie gasped. They might very well be witnessing the most unbalanced swap in the history of school-yard baseball card trading!

But Melina wasn't impressed. "Pass," she said.

"And I'll do your homework for a week," Matt added.

"I can do my own homework," Melina replied. Two strikes for Matt! Oscar and Reggie groaned.

"Name your price," Matt said quickly.

Melina looked him over, sized up the desperation in his eyes, and smiled coldly. "I'll get back to you," she said. With a swish of her blond hair, she walked away.

At seven o'clock the next morning, Lizzie leaped out of bed, threw on her bathrobe, and flew out the door of her bedroom. She bounded down the stairs, overtaking her parents, who were still half asleep.

"Morning, Mom. Morning, Dad," Lizzie sang as she passed them. Flinging open the front door, she snatched up the newspaper on the doorstep. "I love the morning paper," she remarked to her dazed parents. "Don't you just love the morning paper? Isn't the morning paper the best thing in the whole entire world? Yes!"

Clutching the paper to her chest, Lizzie dashed back up the stairs.

Her parents watched her, dumbstruck.

"I was going to read that," Mr. McGuire said. Slowly, he climbed back up the stairs to Lizzie's room. "Could I at least have the sports—"

Slam! Lizzie shut her door. Alone in her room, she shook the paper. An envelope with her name on it fell out onto the bedspread.

Lizzie tore it open. Inside was a note from Ronny.

Dear Lizzie, it started out. *It was so cool to talk with you yesterday. I love the sound of your voice, especially when you laugh. . . .*

Lizzie flopped back on the bed, delirious with happiness.

"i have a boyfriend, a boyfriend, a coolie, coolie, cool boyfriend."

Suddenly, a knock on the door startled Lizzie out of her reverie. *Ugh*—couldn't she have one second of privacy in this house? Grabbing the newspaper, Lizzie opened the door and shoved it into her father's hands. Then she shut the door and curled up on the bed to finish reading Ronny's note.

* * *

Down in the kitchen, Matt was hard at work. He unwrapped sticks of butter, measured out cups of flour and sugar, and briskly stirred them all together in a big ceramic bowl. Measuring cups, sticky spoons, and empty chocolate wrappers littered the counter. A fine layer of flour dust had settled over everything like snow over a disaster site.

His mother shuffled into the kitchen, yawning. But the instant she saw the mess, she was wide-awake. "Um . . . hello?" she said to Matt, who was busily cracking eggs into the bowl.

"We're out of vanilla," Matt said by way of greeting.

Mrs. McGuire scowled. "Are you under the incredibly mistaken impression that you're having brownies for breakfast?" she asked.

"Melina wants freshly baked brownies for lunch today," Matt informed his mother.

"Very sweet of you—" Mrs. McGuire began, heading toward the coffeepot, when suddenly she caught sight of what appeared to be a load of laundry in the kitchen sink. "What's in the sink?" she asked sharply.

"Oh, that's Melina's fine hand-washables," Matt replied. He hurried over to the sink and looked at the sopping clothes. "I think they need a few more minutes."

Just then, Mr. McGuire entered the kitchen, clutching the newspaper. "We're having brownies for breakfast?" he asked, looking hopefully at the mixing bowl.

"Matt, what's going on?" Mrs. McGuire asked.

"Well, Melina has the baseball card I want," Matt explained. "But she'll only give it to me if I meet her demands." He pulled a list from his back pocket and handed it to his mother.

Mr. McGuire leaned over his wife's shoulder to read the list, which was nearly a page long. "That's extortion," he exclaimed.

"That's brilliant," said Mrs. McGuire. "Matt, I'm proud of you, honey. You found something you really want, and you're working hard for it."

"And how," Matt agreed. *Ding!* The egg timer went off. "Oh. Time to feed Melina's snake," he said. "Now where did I put those mice?" Scratching his head, he wandered out of the kitchen.

Mrs. McGuire looked at her husband. "He's kidding, right?" she said.

CHAPTER THREE

Lizzie arrived at school a few minutes early that morning to take care of some important business: redecorating her locker door. Humming to herself, she ripped down the magazine picture of the cute boy band that she'd taped to the door a few months before. Who needed pictures of boy bands when she had a picture of a *real* boyfriend to put in her locker! The day before, Ronny had given her a photo of himself. Lizzie wanted to be able to look at it all day long.

"Is that him?" Miranda asked, when she saw Lizzie taping the photo to her locker door. She moved in for a closer look. "Let me see."

Lizzie stood back, grinning, as Miranda examined the photo of Ronny. He was standing in front of an oleander bush, squinting a little in the sunlight, and he had on the same red T-shirt he'd been wearing the day he told Lizzie he liked her. Lizzie was glad he was wearing that shirt in the photo.

"Cute," Miranda pronounced. "Very cute."

"I know," Lizzie said enthusiastically. "And look, I'm wearing his shoelaces." She lifted her foot so Miranda could see the dirty gray laces woven through the loops of her black boots.

"He said he wanted me to think about him

today," Lizzie explained. "Like, when am I ever not? But I didn't tell him that, because I did just meet him."

Miranda nodded. "That's—"

"And he's making me this tape of all his favorite songs," Lizzie went on, as they headed for math class. "He burns all his own CDs, and he has, like, five hundred hours' worth of music—stop me if I'm talking about him too much," she said to Miranda.

"Actually—" Miranda started to say.

"And I just have to tell you this one thing he said," Lizzie continued. "It's really funny, but it's wise, too. . . ."

Miranda took a deep breath and tried to smile. She could tell it was going to be a long morning.

By lunchtime, Lizzie's monologue was still going strong. Miranda and Gordo sat at the lunch table, numbly chewing their food, as Lizzie babbled on about Ronny's favorite bands, Ronny's favorite TV shows, Ronny's theories on newspaper delivery, and the really hilarious thing that Ronny's best friend's brother said at his mother's cousin's wedding.

"And Ronny was explaining to me how everyone in the world, everyone, is connected by six people. Like somebody who knows somebody who knows somebody who knows somebody who knows Tom Cruise," Lizzie chirped.

"Fascinating," Miranda said, bored out of her mind.

"He just knows tons of cool stuff like that," Lizzie said happily, and launched into a description of exactly how Ronny was connected to Shania Twain and the Dalai Lama!

At last, Miranda had had enough. She pushed her chair back from the table and stood up. "I'm going to get some pudding," she announced.

Gordo leaped up from the table. "Yeah, that sounds good," he said, grateful for any excuse to get away. Together, Miranda and Gordo hurried away from Lizzie, shaking their heads.

Lizzie didn't notice. "Pudding," she said dreamily. "That's a great nickname. Maybe I'll call Ronny 'Pudding.'"

"Do you believe her?" Miranda asked, as she and Gordo walked into the school building. "It's like watching one of those hygiene films they show in health class."

"I guess she really likes him," Gordo said.

"*Likes* him? She's possessed! She's wearing his dirty *shoelaces*!" Miranda flapped her hands in disgust.

"Well, what do you think it is about him?"

Gordo asked. "You think he's a jock? I bet he's a jock."

"Now you're going to talk about him incessantly, too?" Miranda asked impatiently.

"No, it's just . . . so strange," Gordo said. "I mean, other than my parents, Lizzie's the one person I've known my entire life. I guess I never really thought what it would be like when she had a boyfriend."

"Wait, wait." Miranda stopped and looked at Gordo. "Are you *jealous*?"

"Jealous? Oh, no, no, no, no. Wrong road," Gordo said quickly. "I was trying to identify a different emotion. Not jealous."

Miranda nodded, satisfied, and headed off to the cafeteria.

"I think," Gordo added quietly to himself.

Over at the grade school, Matt was following Melina around like a puppy on the end of a leash. So far, he'd baked her brownies, fed her snake, carried her backpack, cleaned her desk, and replaced the missing caps on all her pens—all before noon! At lunchtime, Oscar and Reggie looked on in horror as Melina gave Matt her latest demands.

"I need you to pick up my dry cleaning. This is what I want for lunch today, and see what you can do about these pencils— they're extremely dull," she commanded, handing him two slips of paper and her pencil box.

"Done and done," Matt said.

"She's making you fetch like a dog," Reggie said with disgust. "No baseball card is worth it."

Melina looked coolly at Reggie. "Oh, look," she said suddenly. "There's a spot on my shoe. Matt, could you take care of that for me?"

"Absolutely," said Matt. Pulling a tissue

from his pocket, he fell to his knees and began buffing Melina's shoe.

Reggie and Oscar shook their heads sadly. They never thought they'd see their friend stoop to such lows. "Look away, man," Reggie said, pulling Oscar's sleeve. "Look away."

Lizzie and Ronny had promised to meet at Lizzie's house after school that afternoon. Lizzie thought they might watch TV together, or maybe go over to the Digital Bean. But when Ronny showed up at Lizzie's door, he was holding a pair of Rollerblades and a tiny Polaroid camera. "Want to get some fresh air?" he said, grinning at Lizzie.

Lizzie grinned back, and dashed upstairs to get her own in-line skates. She loved it that Ronny was so spontaneous. They spent the whole afternoon blading up and down Lizzie's block, holding hands, snapping pictures of each other in goofy poses, and crash-landing on other people's lawns. Lizzie had never enjoyed Rollerblading this much.

The sun was almost setting when they finally quit. Laughing and gasping for breath, they bladed over to a bench at the end of the block and sat down. Lizzie's cheeks ached from smiling so much. She wished the day would never end.

"There's something I was kind of wondering about," Ronny said as they sat there.

"What's that?" Lizzie asked.

"Do you consider us boyfriend and girlfriend?"

"I don't know," Lizzie said, suddenly flustered. Of course, she thought he was her boyfriend, but—but what if he didn't think she was his girlfriend? If she said yes, she might totally humiliate herself. But if she said no, he might think she didn't like him! "Do you?" she asked finally.

Ronny smiled. "I asked you first," he said.

"But I think you asked me because you're looking for a certain answer," Lizzie replied carefully. "And I don't want to give you the wrong one."

"Yeah, but if I tell you what I'm thinking, I don't want to look stupid," Ronny said.

Now Lizzie smiled, too. "Me, neither," she said.

"One of us has to say something," Ronny said. For a moment they looked at each other. Lizzie smiled and pressed her lips together tightly.

"Well, it's not going to be me."

"But I guess you should know," he continued slowly, "I told my friends you were my girlfriend."

"Hallelujah!"

"Is that okay?" Ronny asked.

Is that okay? Lizzie thought. Is the sky blue? Is water wet? Is my heart beating like a million miles a minute right now? "Yes," she said.

Ronny reached into his pocket. "Then would you . . . would you consider wearing this?" He pulled out a silver ring and held it out to Lizzie. "It's all silver, so it won't turn your finger green or anything," he said.

Lizzie took the ring and slipped it on her finger. She looked at Ronny. He looked into her eyes. Their faces were very close. Suddenly, Lizzie knew what was about to happen, and her breath caught in her chest.

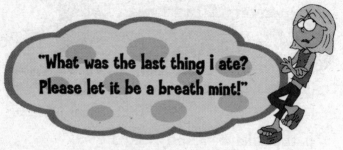

"What was the last thing i ate? Please let it be a breath mint!"

Then Ronny pressed his lips against hers. The kiss lasted for what felt like forever.

When they pulled apart, everything seemed different. Lizzie felt the cool evening air on her cheeks and heard the rustle of the leaves overhead. She noticed the way the sunset turned the white houses pink and saw the little flecks of gold in Ronny's sleepy green eyes. She felt like she was seeing everything for the first time.

But she didn't see Gordo. He was standing

a few feet behind them, clutching a CD he'd made for Lizzie. He'd been on his way to Lizzie's house to give it to her, when he saw her sitting on the bench with Ronny.

Gordo watched as Ronny leaned in for another kiss. His feet felt frozen to the sidewalk. This time there was no mistaking the emotion he was feeling. He was jealous.

CHAPTER FOUR

Lizzie knew what it meant to be on cloud nine. After her date with Ronny, she felt like she was floating in the highest reaches of the atmosphere. Arriving home, she dropped her skates by the front door and sailed through the living room. It was like she was still Rollerblading—her feet hardly seemed to touch the ground. As she passed Matt, who was watching TV, she tousled his hair in a loving way. Matt nearly fell off the sofa in shock.

Humming a love song, Lizzie waltzed into the kitchen and took a can of soda from the refrigerator. Mr. and Mrs. McGuire looked up from the kitchen table, where they were paying bills. They noticed the dazed look on Lizzie's face.

"Are you okay?" Mrs. McGuire asked.

"Oh!" Lizzie exclaimed. "Everything is absolutely, positively, completely, and totally perfect."

Mr. McGuire frowned. "I don't like the sound of that," he said.

"So you had a good time with Ronny?" Mrs. McGuire asked.

"Only the best, most awesome time of my entire life," Lizzie answered dreamily.

"Okay, I *really* don't like the sound of *that*," Mr. McGuire said, leaping to his feet.

"Oh, Sam," Mrs. McGuire said. "He's a nice boy, he's got a job, and they're just friends. It's not like they're going steady or anything—right, Lizzie?"

Rrrrrrrrip! The love song playing in Lizzie's head screeched to a halt, and Lizzie did a half gainer off cloud nine into the land of Busted. Quickly, she hid the hand with Ronny's ring on it behind her back and gave her parents a sickly smile.

"i have the right to remain silent. Anything i say can and will be used against me in a court of law—hmm, i'm watching too many cop shows."

"Lizzie?" her mother said sternly.

"You know what, it's not that big of a deal, and you said yourself he's a nice guy with a job," Lizzie blurted out. "And today he gave me a . . . a *friendship* ring."

Lizzie's parents gasped. Mrs. McGuire clutched her throat. Mr. McGuire's face turned red.

"Let's not panic," said Mrs. McGuire.

"Too late," Mr. McGuire declared. "I think I just burst a blood vessel."

"FYI, Dad, every girl in my grade has a boyfriend—" Lizzie began.

"Does Miranda have a boyfriend?" Mrs. McGuire asked.

First the accusation, now a cross-examination. What were they going to do next, Lizzie wondered. Take her away in handcuffs? "No, Miranda doesn't have a boyfriend," she answered.

"So much for *that* argument," said Mr. McGuire.

"Okay, so I can't have a boyfriend because Miranda doesn't have one?" Lizzie snapped.

"No," her father replied. "Your mother and I feel that—"

"You're doing all the talking here," Mrs. McGuire interrupted, giving him a look.

Mr. McGuire pulled her aside. "I really think it's important we're united on this," he whispered.

"Yeah, but the number one way to make a boy even more appealing to a girl is to tell her she can't see him," Mrs. McGuire whispered back.

"I am not prepared to use reverse psychology here," Mr. McGuire said. "I don't even understand regular psychology."

Lizzie watched her parents with exasperation. Then, throwing her hands in the air, she stormed out of the kitchen.

Miranda wanted to strangle Lizzie. It was Saturday afternoon, and they were supposed to be at the mall an hour ago. But when Miranda arrived at Lizzie's house, Lizzie was on the phone with Ronny. One hour and fifteen minutes later, she was still talking. Miranda lay on Lizzie's bed, staring at the ceiling in a stupor of boredom.

"Cold," she heard Lizzie say into the phone. "Freezing . . . North Pole . . ."

Miranda sat up. "Lizzie," she interrupted. "The mall is closing in five hours."

Lizzie held up a finger, indicating she'd be off in one minute. "Ronny," she said into the phone, "I gotta go. Okay?" She listened for a moment. "No, you hang up first," she said, laughing. "I'm not hanging up first. It's your turn to hang up first. You go first. I'm not hanging up first. You hang up first. . . ."

Click. Suddenly, the line went dead. "R— Ronny?' Lizzie said. She glanced down at the phone. Miranda's finger was on the hang-up button. "Miranda!" Lizzie cried.

"Oh, I'm sorry," Miranda said sarcastically. "I thought you were talking to me."

"Let me just call him back real fast so he doesn't think I hung up on him," Lizzie said. She started to dial his number.

Miranda yanked the phone out of her hands. "Lizzie," she said. "I want you to listen carefully to me." Miranda took a chocolate cookie from a package on Lizzie's desk. "This is your brain," she said, placing the cookie on a book. "And this is your brain on Ronny." Miranda brought her fist down on the cookie, smashing it to bits. "Okay?" she shouted. "You are losing it. A few days ago, this guy was a complete stranger to you. Now he's all you talk about, he's all you think about, he's all you *care* about."

"She has a point."

"That's not true—" Lizzie started to say.

"Oh?" Miranda strode over to Lizzie's desk and picked up a green spiral notebook. "Exhibit A: your history notebook."

"Can I have that back, please?" Lizzie snapped.

Miranda flipped through the pages. "Take any notes yesterday?" she asked.

"Miranda, that's none of your business," Lizzie said. She lunged for the notebook, but Miranda held it out of her reach.

"Oh, yeah, a very productive day," Miranda said. "You have four pages filled out with his name."

Lizzie felt her throat tighten with anger.

Why was everybody so against her dating Ronny? "You never cared what was in my notebook before!" she shouted. "And the only reason you care now is because I have a boyfriend and you don't."

Miranda's face froze. Lizzie sucked in her breath.

"Rewind! Rewind!"

As soon as the words were out of her mouth, Lizzie wished she could take them back. "That came out all wrong—" she said.

"No, I think it came out perfectly. I don't have a boyfriend at the moment," Miranda said, her mouth crumpling with hurt. "And I don't have much of a best friend, either." Grabbing her purse, Miranda stormed out the door.

CHAPTER FIVE

Saturday afternoon, Matt stood on Melina's doorstep, looking like he'd been run over by a garbage truck. His clothes were grass stained and rumpled, his hair stood on end, and his hands and face were streaked with paint. He'd been up since six in the morning, mowing Melina's lawn, fixing her walkway, repainting her address on the sidewalk, and washing her annoying, smelly dogs. He was dirty, tired, sweaty—and happy. Because now he was about to get his reward.

"That's it, I did everything on your list," he told Melina. "The card is mine."

Melina held out the Paul O'Neill card by the tips of her fingers. But as Matt reached for it, she suddenly jerked her hand away. "I've been thinking," she said.

Matt groaned. "That's never good," he said.

"Is it really a fair trade?" Melina asked. "You'll have the entire Yankee roster, but what will I have?"

Matt counted on his fingers. "A washed dog, a cut lawn, a fed snake, clean clothes, delicious brownies, and my undying gratitude."

"True . . ." Melina held out the card. But before Matt could touch it, she yanked it away again. A wicked smile spread across her face. "But I'd like just one more thing," she said.

* * *

A short time later, Matt and his father sat on the McGuires' couch, admiring Matt's baseball card collection. Matt carefully smoothed down the page with the Paul O'Neill card. He'd never seen anything so beautiful in his life.

"I'm proud of you son," Mr. McGuire said. "You worked hard, and you achieved your dream."

"And let me tell you, it wasn't easy," Matt replied. "That Melina is one tough negotiator."

"If you'd like to see a real collection, let me show you mine," Mr. McGuire said. He opened a cabinet and began rooting through a stack of albums. "I've got Roberto Clemente's rookie card . . . Willie Mays, the year he was starting to put chicken on the hill . . ." He dug deeper into the pile. "I know they're in here somewhere—has anyone seen my baseball cards?"

But the cards were gone. Suddenly, Mr. McGuire realized that Matt was suspiciously quiet. He turned and looked at his son.

"Matt?"

"Yes?"

"Where are my cards?" Mr. McGuire asked.

Matt smiled nervously. "Did I mention that Melina's a tough negotiator?" he said.

"You gave her my cards? You gave her *all* my cards? All of them?" Mr. McGuire said with a whimper. "Every single one?"

Matt began to sweat. "Think back, Dad, a minute ago—how proud you were of me," he said.

Mr. McGuire took a deep breath and nodded. "You know, I am proud of you, son. This is a very impressive collection," he said slowly. "And I'm sure it's going to be worth a small fortune someday!" he added, snatching up Matt's cards. Tucking the binder under his arm, he stormed out of the room.

Just then, the doorbell rang. Lizzie careened down the stairs, yelling, "I'll get it! I'll get it! I'll get it!" Checking her reflection quickly in the hallway mirror, she flung open the door. Ronny was standing on the doorstep. "Hey," Lizzie said.

"Hi," said Ronny.

Before they could say more, Mr. McGuire suddenly charged up to the door and slapped a folded bill into Ronny's hand. "Is this what you came for, paperboy?" he growled. Lizzie wanted to crawl under the sofa and die of humiliation.

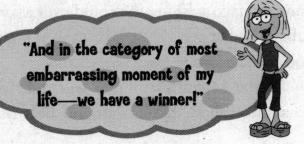

"And in the category of most embarrassing moment of my life—we have a winner!"

Fortunately, Mrs. McGuire came to the rescue. "Back off, tiger," she said, putting her hand on her husband's arm. Gently, she pulled him away from the door.

But suddenly, she heard Ronny say to Lizzie, "Can you come out? We need to talk." Mrs. McGuire froze. She didn't like the sound of that.

Lizzie turned to her parents. "Can I, Mom? Please?"

Mrs. McGuire gave her a worried look. "Lizzie, I don't know if you should."

"Mom, please? Please, please, please, please, *pleeeeeeease*?" Lizzie begged.

Mrs. McGuire looked at her daughter's hopeful face, wishing she could stop what was about to happen. "Just take care of yourself, okay?" she said at last.

Maybe Miranda's mother was right about that full moon, Lizzie thought, because her parents were being seriously abnormal. "This is even weirder than their normal weirdness," Lizzie told Ronny as she followed him outside.

When they were gone, Mrs. McGuire sighed. "Oh, man. Our daughter is about to have her heart broken," she said sadly.

"What? Who? Where?" Mr. McGuire exclaimed. "Nobody ever tells me anything."

"He just said, 'We need to talk,'" Mrs. McGuire explained. "Those are the four most horrible words in the English language. Nothing good ever follows 'we need to talk.'"

Outside, Lizzie and Ronny walked down the block. Lizzie wished Ronny would hold her hand like he had when they were Rollerblading. But Ronny kept his hands in his pockets and stared at the ground as he walked. He didn't say anything.

"I mean, I don't know if you celebrate Valentine's Day," Lizzie chattered. Ronny's silence was making her uncomfortable. "I was just saying, if you did . . ."

"Okay," Ronny said flatly.

"I know it's, like, totally doofy and everything," Lizzie continued, "but, you know, there are all these cards and stuff—"

Ronny stopped walking. "Lizzie . . . something's happened," he said.

"What is it? Is it bad?" she asked.

"I don't know," Ronny said. "I'm not . . . I'm not sure about some stuff."

"Uh-huh," Lizzie said nervously. She was starting to have a bad feeling about this conversation.

"See, it turns out that there's . . . there's this girl at my school who likes me. She's right there and everything." Ronny looked at the ground again. "I just don't know if right now is the best time for me to have a girlfriend."

"Oh." Lizzie felt like someone was squeezing her chest.

"This really, really hurts."

"You like her, too?" she asked.

"Well, you know . . . yeah. But I still like you." Ronny had a pained look on his face. "Maybe I shouldn't have given you that ring. . . . But you can keep it if you want," he added quickly.

"No, no," Lizzie said, already tugging it off her finger.

"I bought it for you," Ronny said.

"That's okay. I don't want it." Lizzie dropped the ring into his hand. She couldn't look at him. Her eyes began to fill with tears.

"We can still be friends, can't we?" Ronny asked.

Lizzie looked at him in disbelief, the tears starting to spill over. Without a word, she turned and walked away.

"Lizzie . . ." Ronny said, reaching for her arm.

Lizzie kept walking, wiping at her eyes.

"I'm really sorry," Ronny said behind her.

Lizzie broke into a run. She wanted to get away from him as fast as possible. Without looking back, she ran all the way home.

Mr. and Mrs. McGuire were in the living room when they heard the front door open. Lizzie bolted past them up the stairs.

"Lizzie?" Mrs. McGuire called gently.

Slam! The door to Lizzie's room banged shut.

"I should go talk to her, right?" Mr. McGuire asked.

Mrs. McGuire shook her head. "There's nothing we can say."

CHAPTER SIX

At lunchtime on Monday, Lizzie sat in a back corner of the school library, tearing Ronny out of her heart—or at least out of her notebook. One by one, she ripped out the pages she had filled with Ronny's name. Then she tore those pages into little pieces. Soon there was a mound of shredded paper on the table. Lizzie stared at the pile. She felt a little better. But not much.

Suddenly, she heard someone ask, "Is there a confetti shortage?"

Lizzie looked up. Gordo was watching her with concern.

"Not anymore," Lizzie said, wiping at the tears that sprang up in her eyes.

"I missed you at lunch today," Gordo said.

Lizzie sniffled. "I'm not very hungry."

Gordo pulled out a chair and sat down next to her. "They got the big chocolate-chip cookies," he said. "I got one for you." He held it out to her.

"Thanks," she said, taking the cookie. She set it next to the pile of paper. For a moment, no one said anything. At last, Lizzie sighed tearily. "Ronny broke up with me," she told Gordo.

"He's a loser," Gordo replied.

"No, Gordo, I'm the loser. Okay?" Lizzie cried. "He likes another girl. She's probably prettier than me. She's probably smarter than me, and she's probably a lot more fun than I am."

"No, she's not," said Gordo.

"How do you know?" Lizzie asked.

Gordo looked at her and smiled. "Because there is nobody prettier than you, or more fun to be with," he said.

"You forgot 'smarter,'" Lizzie said.

"Yeah, well, I was including myself in that one."

Lizzie half smiled, even though she was still crying. "I feel so awful," she admitted.

"Yeah, I know," Gordo said. "But you'll get over it. Whereas that guy? He's going to realize what an idiot he was, and he's going to feel awful the rest of his life."

The fifth-period bell rang, signaling that it was time for class to begin. Lizzie took a deep breath, and discovered she really did feel better. "You're such a good friend, Gordo," she said.

"Yeah, well . . ." Gordo paused.

"What?" Lizzie asked, seeing the look on his face.

Gordo stood up. He frowned as if he were considering something.

"Gordo, what?" Lizzie asked again.

He shook his head. "Nothing," he said. "Nothing."

Lizzie shrugged. "Okay."

She picked up her schoolbooks.

Just then, Miranda walked into the library. As soon as she saw Lizzie's face, she knew what had happened. Without a word, she hugged Lizzie to say she was sorry. Lizzie hugged her back to say she was sorry, too. Then, with their arms around each other's shoulders, the three friends walked to class.